Hairs on Bears

Text by Geraldine Ryan-Lush
Illustrations by Normand Cousineau

Annick Press
Toronto • New York

Annick Press gratefully acknowledges the support
of the Canada Council and the Ontario Arts Council.

Canadian Cataloguing in Publication Data
Ryan-Lush, Geraldine, 1949-
Hairs on bears

ISBN 1-55037-351-X (bound) ISBN 1-55037-352-8 (pbk.)

I. Cousineau, Normand. II. Title.
PS8585.Y37H35 1994   jC813'.54 C94-930729-7
PZ7.R8Ha 1994

The art in this book was rendered in gouache and inks.
The text was typeset in Trump Mediæval.

Distributed in Canada by:
Firefly Books Ltd.
250 Sparks Ave.
Willowdale, ON M2H 2S4

Published in the U.S.A. by Annick Press (U.S.) Ltd.
Distributed in the U.S.A. by:
Firefly Books Ltd.
P.O. Box 1338
Ellicott Station
Buffalo, NY 14205

Printed on acid-free paper.
Printed and bound in Canada by
D.W. Friesen & Sons, Altona, Manitoba.

For Shannon and
Barrie and Scamp,
who inspired it
G.R.L.

For Monique and
Marie-Louise
N.C.

Hairs on fingers
Hairs on toes
Hairs right up
    Aunt Bertha's nose
    (AA-CHOO!)
Now you see them
Now you don't
Now guests come
    and now they won't

Hairs on blankets
Hairs on chairs
Hairs on bureaus
Hairs on bears
Hairs on Mom –
    she throws a fit –
Where's the dog?
Get rid of it!

Hairs on sweaters
Hairs on suits
Hairs on
   Uncle Watson's boots
Hairs on zippers
Hairs on pleats
Hairs on ladies
   and their seats
Hairs float up and
   hairs float down
Hairs on
   Mr. Sherman's crown

Hairs on slippers
Hairs on socks
Hairs on Lego
Hairs on locks
Hairs on pictures
Hairs on desks
Hairs on Grandpa's mouth.
What pests!

Dog, you are no
    doggone good
I should sell you –
    yes I should

Hairs on vases
Hairs on books
Hairs on butlers
Hairs on cooks
Hairs are floating
Hairs are still
Hairs are on
    your window sill

We must catch them
We must try
We must send them
    to the sky
Mom is sneezing
Dad is sick
We must clean
    those hairs – and quick

Get the vacuum
Hear it roar
It will clean up
  hairs on floor
It will clean
  Aunt Bertha's hat
Nice and fluffy –
  she'll like that!

Clean the ceiling
Clean the door
We won't see those hairs
  no more
Clean the lampshade
Clean the couch
Clean old Winston's
  wet nose – ouch!
Clean the fridge
  and TV too
Hey! I know
  just what to do

This vacuum cleaner,
  it's too small
We need a bigger one,
  that's all
This big thing here
  should do the trick
It's grabbing up
  those hairs – real quick

It's grabbing
  all the tables too
And chairs and things –
What shall we do?

I don't believe it!
Still hairs on socks
Hairs on Lego
Hairs on locks
Hairs on handbags
Hairs on plants
Hairs on hamsters
Hairs on ants!
Hairs on hairs –
On mittens, too –
I do not know
   just what to do!

Take Dog out and
  brush him down
Walk him, walk him
  through the town
He will give a
  mighty shake –
Just like a
  doggy-powered quake

He will lose those
  hairs, each one
Toward the water
  and the sun
He will lose them –
Never fear –
Until they grow back
  on next year!

But if you brush your dog
   just right
You won't have no
   hairs to fight

We walked him up
We walked him down
We walked him all
   around the town
He gave a heave
He gave a shake
Just like a
   doggy-powered quake

We brushed him hard
We brushed him fast
We brushed him well
Oh, what a blast!

He didn't like it –
Not at all –
He gave a kick,
He gave a growl
But we were stern,
  we had to be,
We had to get him
  clean, you see!

The hairs went up
  into the sky
They seemed to float
They seemed to fly
They fluttered to
  the ocean grand
And on the trees
  they seemed to land

They landed here
They landed there
They landed on
  most everywhere...
Then soared so high
  up to the sky
And, disappearing,
  waved... goodbye!
I watched them flutter
  out of sight
Into the sun
Into the night
They're gone!
  they're gone!
I said to Bill
Come on – let's go
  back down the hill

This dog is one
  clean mutt today
Now guests can come
  and now they'll stay!

RULES:
Use one die and checkers or buttons for markers. Whoever rolls a six begins. Green squares mean advance three; red, go back three; yellow, lose a turn. The first to reach 28 with exactly the right number of moves wins. (For two or more players.)